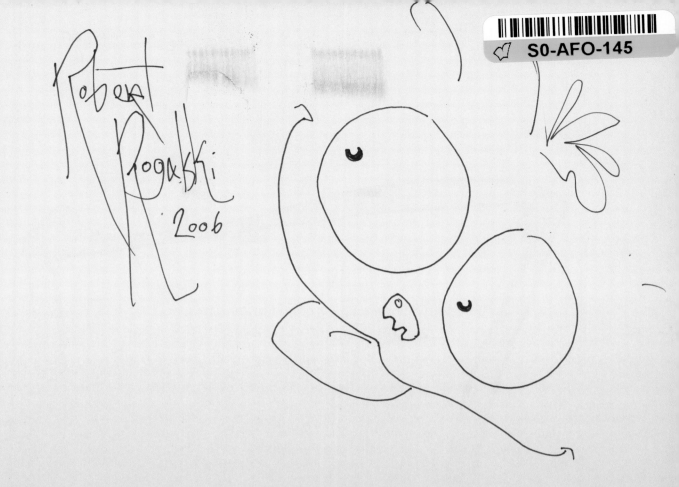

Robert Rogalski
2006

*Dedicated to the innate goodness of humanity
and our ongoing efforts to improve upon it —
also to my mother, Barbara Grace Perry Stutsman,
in her 100th year — EPR*

*To my Mom and Dad —
Thank you for believing in me — RR*

Mrs. Murphy's Marvelous Mansion

By Emma Perry Roberts
Illustrated by Robert Rogalski

ILLUMINATION Arts

PUBLISHING COMPANY, INC.
Bellevue, Washington
www.illumin.com

Mrs. Murphy lived on a very fine street, in a very fine neighborhood, in a very fine town. She was a very fine person. When Mrs. Murphy took her dog, Pickles, for a walk she would greet everyone with a smile and say, "Have a very fine day!"

The neighbors always watched
with amazement when Mrs. Murphy returned
from her walk and entered her house. It looked so small they
wondered how she could move around once she got inside. They did not like
the odd little house. In fact, they tried to pretend it wasn't there at all.

One very fine day, when Mrs. Murphy left her house, she found the neighbors gathered around a large billboard.

Chattering with excitement, they each
offered ideas on how to make their neighborhood
even more beautiful.

"Let's put up a grand welcome sign," said Mr. Brown.

"And elegant lamp posts on every corner," added Ms. Black.

"Let's add trees and flowers along the sidewalks," said
Mrs. Green, "and park benches with a fountain in the circle."

"We must include a magnificent statue!" declared Mr. Gold.

"What very fine ideas," observed Mrs. Murphy with a cheerful smile.

As soon as she walked away,
the neighbors began complaining about
Mrs. Murphy's peculiar little house.

"Her house is really ugly," muttered Ms. Black.

"It's barely bigger than a cracker box!" said Mr. Gold.

"We certainly won't win THE VERY FINEST NEIGHBORHOOD CONTEST
with that awful little house on our street," shouted Mr. Brown. "It should
be torn down!"

When Mrs. Murphy returned from
her walk, Mr. Gold called out to her, "We have an
important matter to discuss with you. It's about the
VERY FINEST NEIGHBORHOOD CONTEST."

"And about your house," said Mrs. White. "You see, we think it's not...
well, we just think that..."

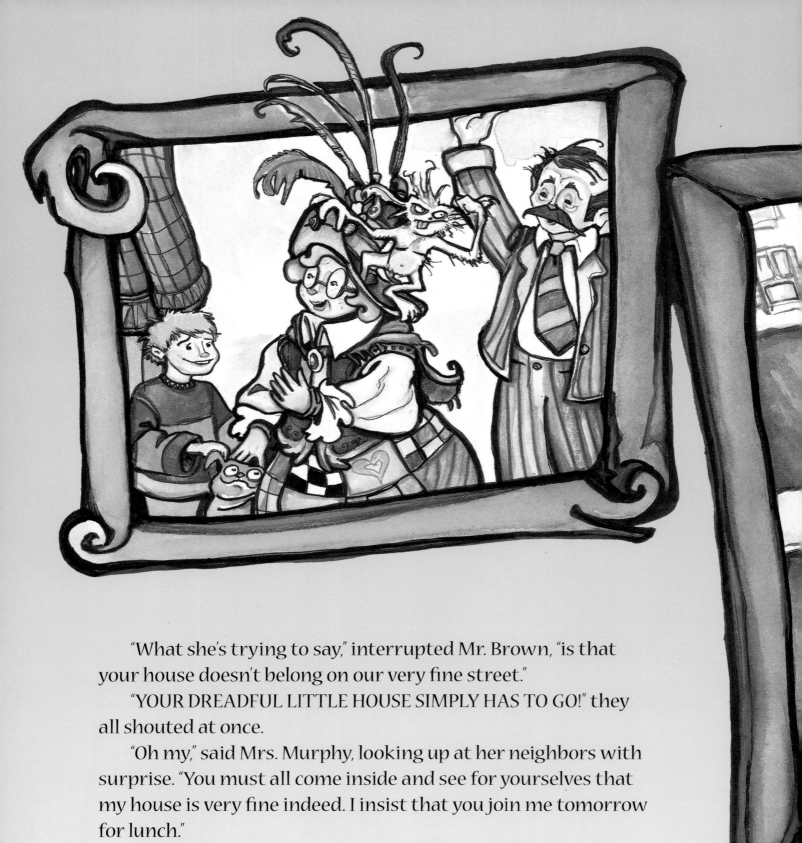

"What she's trying to say," interrupted Mr. Brown, "is that your house doesn't belong on our very fine street."

"YOUR DREADFUL LITTLE HOUSE SIMPLY HAS TO GO!" they all shouted at once.

"Oh my," said Mrs. Murphy, looking up at her neighbors with surprise. "You must all come inside and see for yourselves that my house is very fine indeed. I insist that you join me tomorrow for lunch."

The neighbors looked at one another in astonishment and began to whisper among themselves. Finally Mr. Gold announced, "We have decided to accept your invitation."

The next day, when Mrs. Murphy's neighbors stepped through her peculiar little door, they were flabbergasted. "Your house appears to be quite roomy!" gasped Mr. Brown.

"I do love open spaces," replied Mrs. Murphy.

"Just look at all these doors!" exclaimed Mrs. White.
"With more surprises behind each one," said Mrs. Murphy with a satisfied smile.

"Your home is so full of light!" said Ms. Black.

"And doesn't that make it bright and cheerful," replied Mrs. Murphy.

"This is astonishing!" declared Mrs. Green.
"You have wonderful plants and flowers
everywhere!"
"Why of course," said Mrs. Murphy. "They
add such beauty and color."

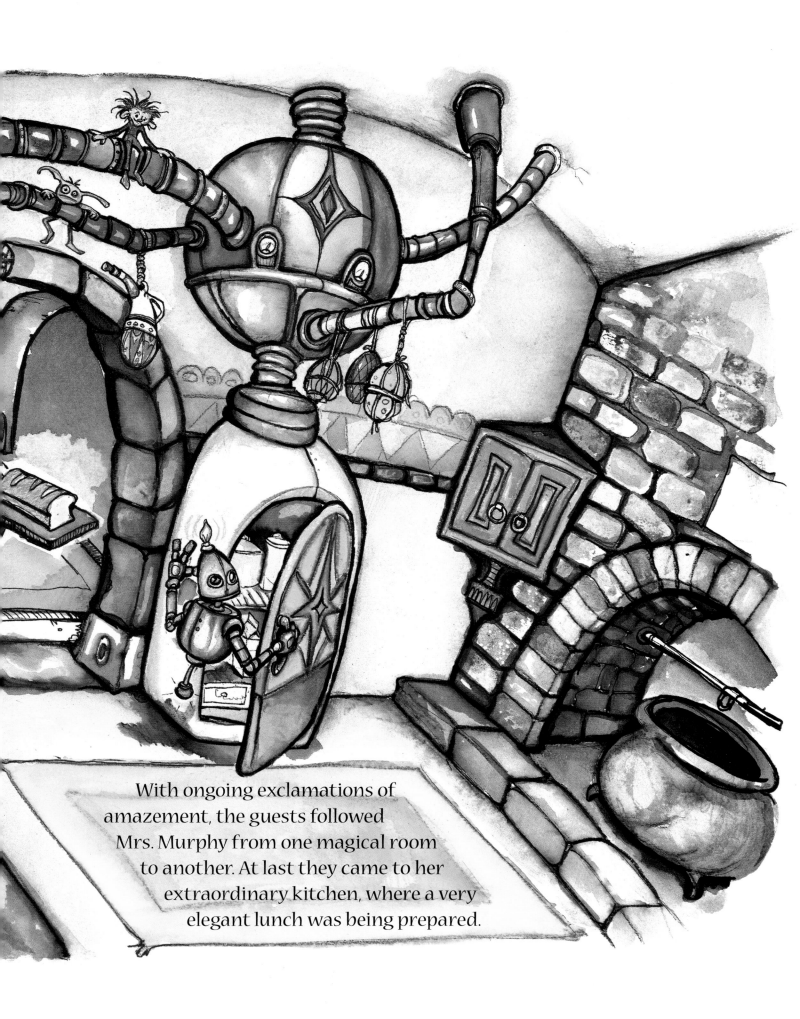

With ongoing exclamations of amazement, the guests followed Mrs. Murphy from one magical room to another. At last they came to her extraordinary kitchen, where a very elegant lunch was being prepared.

Mrs. Murphy's neighbors chattered happily as they ate the mouth-watering meal. The delicacies included cheddar and mushroom quiche, baked yams with honey glaze, and a wild green salad with pine nuts. Next the guests enjoyed Mrs. Murphy's lively entertainment as they feasted upon strawberry-rhubarb pie a la mode. The meal was topped off with a cup of homemade cinnamon tea.

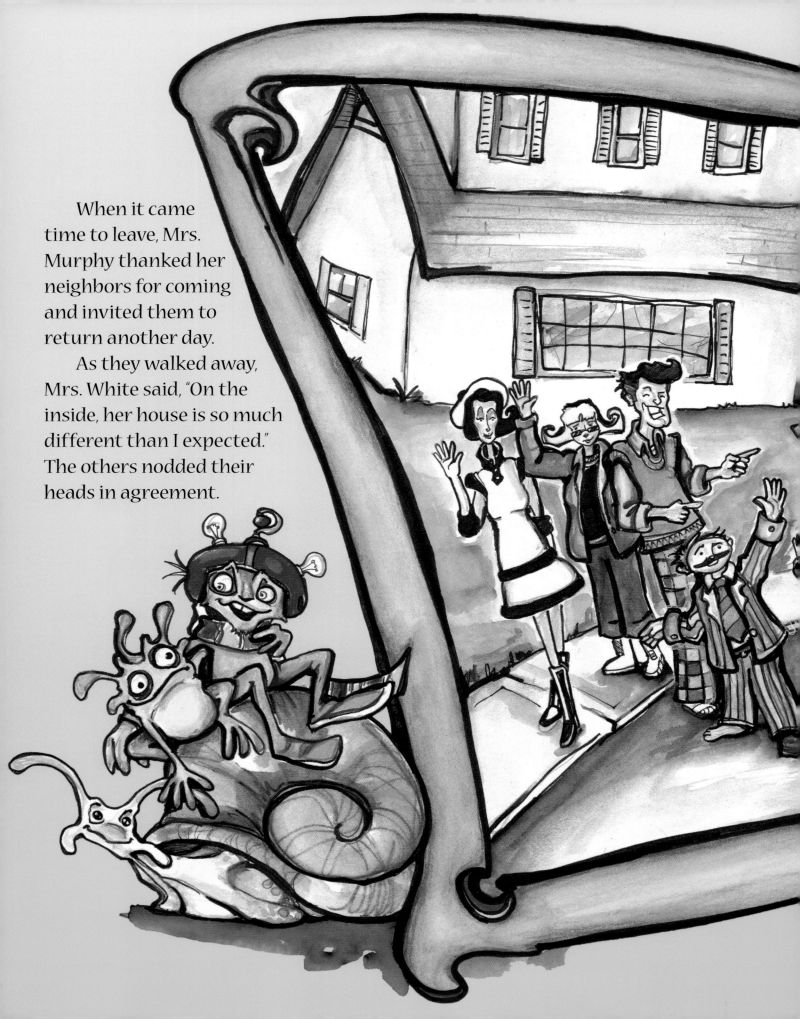

When it came time to leave, Mrs. Murphy thanked her neighbors for coming and invited them to return another day.

As they walked away, Mrs. White said, "On the inside, her house is so much different than I expected." The others nodded their heads in agreement.

"When we looked only at the *outside*," declared
Mr. Brown, "we couldn't appreciate the *inside*."

"But, what about THE VERY FINEST NEIGHBORHOOD CONTEST?" questioned Mr. Gold. "It seems to me that..."

"We already have the very finest neighborhood!" interrupted Mr. Brown.

"AND THE VERY FINEST NEIGHBORS!" the others agreed, as they waved goodbye to Mrs. Murphy.

"It is a very fine day indeed," mused Mrs. Murphy, "when we learn that beauty on the inside matters more than beauty on the outside."

She turned with a smile and entered her very fine house, closing the little door behind her.

PUBLISHING COMPANY, INC.

P.O. Box 1865 • Bellevue, WA 98009

Tel: 425-644-7185 • 888-210-8216 (orders only) • Fax: 425-644-9274

liteinfo@illumin.com • **www.illumin.com**

INSPIRE EVERY CHILD FOUNDATION

A portion of the profits from this book will be donated to Inspire Every Child, a non-profit foundation dedicated to helping disadvantaged children around the world. This organization provides inspirational children's books to individuals and organizations that are directly involved in supporting the welfare of children. The directors and officers of Inspire Every Child provide their services on a voluntary basis, so that donations go directly to help children in need. Your help in supporting this worthwhile cause would be greatly appreciated. Please visit **www.inspire-every-child.org** for more information.

Published in the United States of America

Printed in Singapore by Tien Wah Press

Book Designer: Molly Murrah, Murrah & Company, Kirkland, WA

Illumination Arts Publishing Company, Inc. is a member of Publishers in Partnership –
replanting our nation's forests.

More inspiring picture books from Illumination Arts

Little Yellow Pear Tomatoes
Demian Elainé Yumei/Nicole Tamarin, ISBN 0-9740190-2-X
Ponder the never-ending circle of life through the eyes of a young girl, who marvels at all the energy and collaboration it takes to grow yellow pear tomatoes.

Something Special
Terri Cohlene/Doug Keith, ISBN 0-9740190-1-1
A curious little frog finds a mysterious gift outside his home near the castle moat. It's Something Special…What can it be?

Am I a Color Too?
Heidi Cole/Nancy Vogl/Gerald Purnell, ISBN 0-9740190-5-4
A young interracial boy wonders why people are labeled by the color of their skin. Seeing that people dream, feel, sing, dance and love regardless of their color, he asks, "Am I a color, too?"

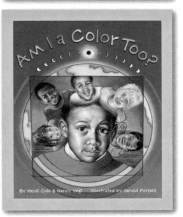

The Tree
Dana Lyons/David Danioth, ISBN 0-9701907-1-9
An urgent call to preserve our fragile environment, The Tree reminds us that hope for a brighter future lies in our own hands.

Too Many Murkles
Heidi Charissa Schmidt/Mary Gregg Byrne, ISBN 0-9701907-7-8
Each spring the people of Summerville gather to prevent the dreaded Murkles from entering their village. Unfortunately, this year there are more of the strange, smelly creatures than ever.

We Share One World
Jane E. Hoffelt/Marty Husted, ISBN 0-9701907-8-6
Wherever we live—whether we work in the fields, the waterways, the mountains or the cities—all people and creatures share one world.

A Mother's Promise
Lisa Humphrey/David Danioth ISBN 0-9701907-9-4
A lifetime of sharing begins with the sacred vow a woman makes to her unborn child.

Your Father Forever
Travis Griffith/Raquel Abreu, ISBN 0-9740190-3-8
A devoted father promises to guide, protect and respect his beloved children. Transcending the boundaries of culture and time, this is the perfect expression of a parent's universal love.

To view our whole collection visit us at www.illumin.com